Jason the Penguin (He's Different)

Written by Deb McEwan
Illustrated by Mary Monette Barbaso-Crall

Jason the Penguin
(He's Different)

Copyright Deb McEwan 2015

To celebrate the birth of Arya Williamson.
You already brighten our world.

On lovely Penguin Island
Where it was bright and warm
The fairy penguins waited
For their babies to be born.

The chicks were oh so tired
They'd been working day and night,
And started hatching from their eggs
To their parents' great delight.

'Eh up,' said Jason penguin
As he stepped out of his shell.
'You must be my mum and dad,
By 'eck you both look well.'

Jason's Mum was happy
But his dad was so confused.
He didn't know what Jason said
Nor any words he'd used.

His father loved him dearly
But vowed to help his son
To sound more like a penguin,
He'd discuss it with his mum.

'Fish for tea,' said Jason's Mum
'Let's catch it,' said his dad.
So off they waddled to the sea
To fetch food for their lad.

The baby penguins tweeted
As their parents brought their fish.
It could be hard to find their own
Amongst big groups like this.

But Jason's parents heard him
From quite a distance off.
'Eh up I'm over here,' he said.
'I hope you've brought my scoff.'

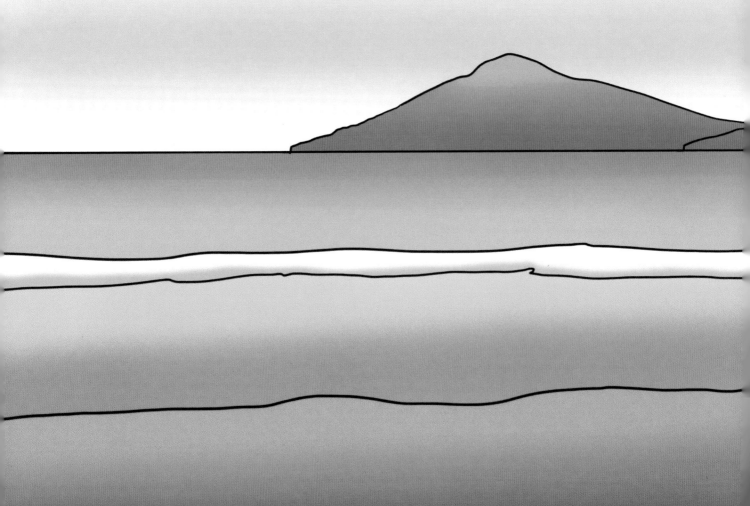

He quickly gobbled up the fish
Then wiped his mouth with glee.
Thanking both his parents
For bringing him his tea.

'That's it,' said Jason's father.
'I don't know what he said,
This could be quite a problem.'
He frowned and scratched his head.

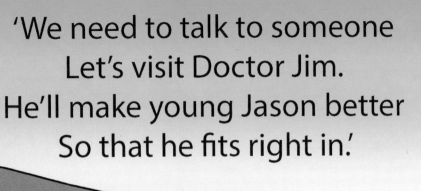

'We need to talk to someone
Let's visit Doctor Jim.
He'll make young Jason better
So that he fits right in.'

The family walked along the beach
And reached the surgery.
While the doctor spoke to Jason,
His parents drank some tea.

'Jason is a lovely lad
He's fit and healthy too.'
The doctor smiled and then he said.
'There's not a lot to do.'

'When he talks to you just listen.'
He looked at Jason's Dad.
'You'll soon pick up his accent
And then you won't feel bad.'

Jason's Dad was happy
Now he knew the day would come,
When he would learn the words of Yorkshire
And could understand his son.

His mum said, 'Jason's special.'
She bent and rubbed his head.
'He's also very tired.
It's time he went to bed.'

They read his bedtime story,
Then Jason closed his eyes.
Not knowing that the next day
He was in for a surprise!

Message from the Author

We received the joyful news on Christmas Day 2014
that our lovely niece Rebecca and her wonderful husband
Craig were expecting their first baby.

They asked if I'd write a book to celebrate the birth,
telling me that Craig liked penguins (subtle eh?).
That's how the idea for *Jason the Penguin* was hatched.
Arya Williamson was born a little earlier than expected
on 25 April 2015.

Thank you to Monette for her wonderful illustrations, and thank you for purchasing and reading this book. I'd be grateful if you'd consider leaving a review at Amazon. If your little one enjoyed it you may like the next one *Jason the Penguin (He Learns to Swim)*. For further information, please check out my website at

www.debbiemcewansbooks.com.
I love to hear from readers so if you'd like to contact me here's my email deborahmcewan@yahoo.co.uk

Printed in Great
Britain
by Amazon

32252514R00015